For
Noah x

tiger tales

An imprint of ME Media LLC
202 Old Ridgefield Road
Wilton, CT 06897
First published in the United States 2001
Originally published in Great Britain 2001
by Little Tiger Press, London
Text and Illustrations ©2001 Tim Warnes
ISBN 1-58925-010-9
CIP data available
First US Edition
Printed in Italy

Can't you sleep, Dotty?

★ ★ ★

Tim Warnes

tiger tales

Dotty couldn't sleep.
It was her first night in
her new home.

She tried sleeping
upside down.

She tried
snuggling up
to Penguin.

She even
tried lying on
the floor.

AWOOOOOOOOoooo

But still Dotty
couldn't sleep.

Dotty's howling woke up Pip the Mouse. "Can't you sleep, Dotty?" he asked. "Perhaps you should try counting the stars like I do."

But Dotty
could only count
up to one. *That*
wasn't enough to
send her to sleep.

What could she do next?

AWOOOOOOOOOO

Susie the Bird was awake now. "Can't you sleep, Dotty?" she chirped. "I always have a little drink before I go to bed."

Chirp!

Chirp!

Dotty went to her bowl
and had a little drink.

Slurp!
Slurp!

But then she made a tiny puddle. Well *that* wouldn't help! What *could* Dotty do to get to sleep?

AWOOOOOOOO . . .

Whiskers the Rabbit had woken up, too. "Can't you sleep, Dotty?" he mumbled sleepily. "I hide in my den at bedtime. That always works."

Dotty dived under her blanket so that only her bottom was showing. But it was very dark under there with no light at all.

Boing!

Dotty was too scared to go to sleep.

AWOOOOOOOOOOooooo

Flump!

Tommy the Tortoise
poked his head from
out of his shell.

"Can't you sleep, Dotty?" he sighed. "I like
to sleep where it's bright and sunny."

Dotty liked the idea...

and turned on her flashlight!

"Turn it off, Dotty!"
shouted all her friends.
"*We* can't get to sleep now!"

Poor Dotty was too tired to try
anything else. Then Tommy had
a great idea!

He helped Dotty into her bed.
What Dotty needed for the first
night in her new home was...

to snuggle among *all* her
new friends. Soon they
were all fast asleep.

Good night, Dotty.